Earth-Friendly Transportation

Miriam Coleman

PowerKiDS press.

New York

Published in 2011 by The Rosen Publishing Group, Inc.
29 East 21st Street, New York, NY 10010

First Edition

Editor: Joanne Randolph
Book Design: Kate Laczynski

Photo Credits: Cover Darrin Klimek/Getty Images; p. 4 Creatas Images/Creatas/Thinkstock; p. 5 Jupiterimages/Polka Dot/Thinkstock; pp. 6, 14, 15, 21, 26 Shutterstock.com; p. 7 Tim Graham/Getty Images; pp. 8–9 DC Productions/Valueline/Thinkstock; p. 10 Thinkstock Images/Comstock/Thinkstock; pp. 11, 12 Matthias Hiekel/AFP/Getty Images; p. 13 Car Culture/Getty Images; pp. 16–17 iStockphoto/Thinkstock; p. 18 Thomas Coex/AFP/Getty Images; p. 19 Darren McCollester/Getty Images; p. 20 Altrendo Travel/Getty Images; p. 22 David McNew/Getty Images; p. 23 Digital Vision/Thinkstock; p. 24 Don Emmert/AFP/Getty Images; p. 25 Stephen Brashear/Getty Images; p. 27 Jonathan Alcorn/Bloomberg/Getty Images; p. 28 Yoshikazu Tsuno/AFP/Getty Images; p. 29 Volker Hartmann/AFP/Getty Images; p. 30 Roger Weber/Digital Vision/Thinkstock.

Library of Congress Cataloging-in-Publication Data

Coleman, Miriam.
 Earth-friendly transportation / by Miriam Coleman. — 1st ed.
   p. cm. — (How to be Earth friendly)
 Includes index.
 ISBN 978-1-4488-2590-5 (library binding) — ISBN 978-1-4488-2769-5 (pbk.) — ISBN 978-1-4488-2770-1 (6-pack)
 1. Transportation—Environmental aspects—Juvenile literature. I. Title.
 HE147.65.C65 2011
 388.3—dc22
                              2010036208

Manufactured in the United States of America

CPSIA Compliance Information: Batch #WW11PK: For Further Information contact Rosen Publishing, New York, New York at 1-800-237-9932

CONTENTS

What Is Earth-Friendly Transportation?

Cars, trains, planes, and buses move people around the world. They take us to work and on vacations. They bring us to school and to visit friends and relatives. **Transportation** keeps the world moving! It can also hurt the **environment**, though. Cars, trains, and buses need **fuel** to run. Often these fuels are made

Taking the subway is an Earth-friendly way to get around. Subway trains can carry hundreds of people. That means those people are not driving cars.

We fill cars up with gas at gas stations. Our cars' engines burn that gas to make the cars run. Burning the fuel puts harmful matter into the air.

from natural **resources** that cannot be replaced. Burning these fuels causes pollution in the air and water, too. To keep Earth healthy, we need less harmful ways to get around.

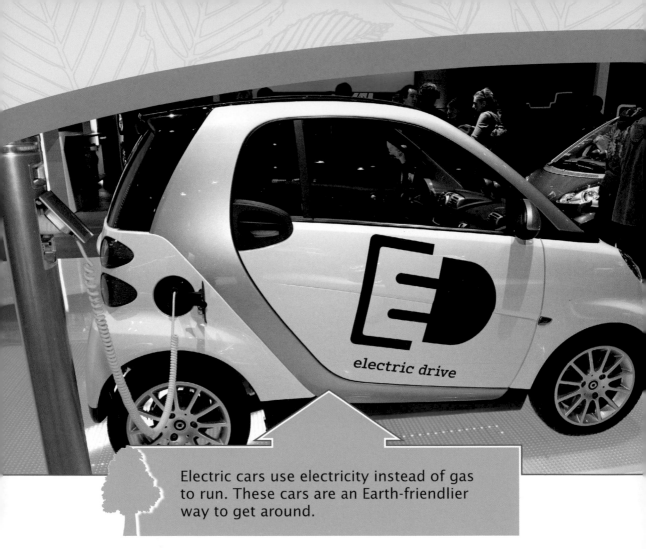

Electric cars use electricity instead of gas to run. These cars are an Earth-friendlier way to get around.

Earth-friendly, or green, transportation is **sustainable**. This means that it uses natural resources in a way that will continue to support people in the future. Earth-friendly transportation tries to use fuel **efficiently** and reduce pollution. What can you do to help Earth?

What's Wrong with the Old Way?

City streets are often crowded with cars and buses. All of these vehicles are putting carbon dioxide into the air.

Most **vehicles** today run on gasoline or diesel fuel, which are made from petroleum. Petroleum is a fossil fuel. This means that it was formed from plant or animal matter over millions of years. One problem with fossil fuels is that they are nonrenewable, which means that we cannot make more when we run out. The search for more petroleum leads companies to drill for oil in wilderness areas and in the ocean. This drilling is not good for the natural environment.

Vehicle engines burn the petroleum to get power from it. The pollution from this can cause breathing problems in some people. Burning petroleum

This offshore drilling platform is used to drill for oil beneath the ocean floor. Underwater drilling can cause leaks that hurt nearby plants and animals.

also produces very large amounts of a gas called **carbon dioxide**. Carbon dioxide is known as a greenhouse gas. When it collects in the atmosphere, it traps heat near

Earth's surface in the same way that a glass greenhouse holds in heat. Scientists call this the greenhouse effect. We count on the greenhouse effect to keep Earth warm enough for us to live here. However, too much carbon dioxide in the air is causing Earth to get too warm.

If we can stop burning so much petroleum to get around, we can make a big difference in fighting global warming and air pollution. We can also make the world's supply of oil last longer.

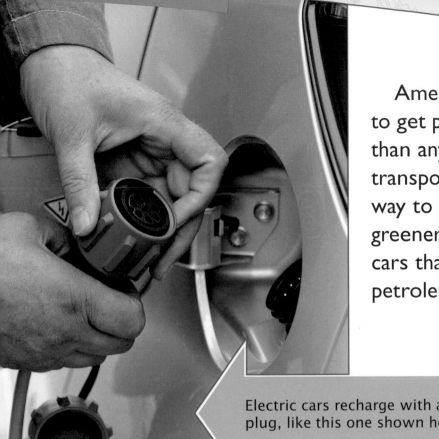

Americans use cars to get places more than any other type of transportation. One way to make travel greener is by creating cars that can use less petroleum fuel.

Electric cars recharge with a special plug, like this one shown here.

The electric car uses no petroleum at all. Instead of burning fuel from a gas tank, an electric car has a **battery** that powers the car with electricity. Electric cars create almost no air pollution as they run. Current models of electric cars must be recharged every 50 to 100 miles

(80–161 km), though. It takes a long time to recharge them. Another problem with electric cars is how you get the electricity. If you plug them into an ordinary home **outlet**, the

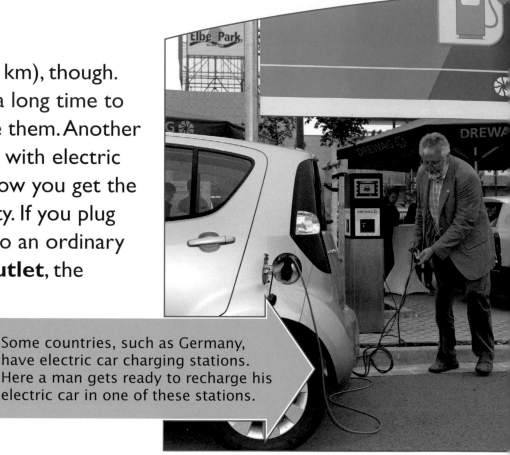

Some countries, such as Germany, have electric car charging stations. Here a man gets ready to recharge his electric car in one of these stations.

electricity often comes from a power plant that produces just as much air pollution and carbon dioxide as a regular car. If the energy could come from a clean source, such as solar or wind power, electric cars would have huge benefits for the environment.

Hybrid cars combine energy from a gasoline engine with electricity generated by a battery. The motion of the car feeds electricity to the battery so you do not need to plug the car into an electric outlet to charge it. This means that you can drive it as you would an

Hybrid cars, such as this one, still use petroleum-based fuel. They use much less of it than regular cars do, though.

Many car companies are now working on making plug-in hybrid cars. These cars use ideas from electric and hybrid cars, so they use even less gas.

ordinary car and fill it up with gas at regular gas stations. Hybrid cars use about two-thirds the amount of fuel that ordinary cars do. Many carmakers now offer hybrid models alongside their regular cars.

Growing Renewable Fuel

Brazil grows a lot of sugar. In the 1930s, Brazil started using sugarcane to produce ethanol. Ethanol is now widely used as fuel in Brazil. It is produced in ways that do not harm the environment as corn does here. Many cars in Brazil are even made to run on ethanol alone.

This is an ethanol plant in South Dakota. It uses corn to make fuel.

Scientists are trying to find ways to reduce the use of nonrenewable fossil fuels. One way to do this is to power cars using fuel that we can grow. Fuel made from plants and other organic matter is called biofuel. There are three main kinds of biofuel. These are bioalcohol, biodiesel, and biogas.

Bioalcohols are made by **fermenting** the sugars in plants. The most common type of bioalcohol is ethanol, which can be mixed in small amounts with gasoline and used in ordinary gasoline engines. Flex-fuel cars can use any combination of ethanol and gasoline. Bioethanol burns cleaner than gasoline or diesel. Unfortunately, most ethanol in the United States is made from corn. Corn takes a lot of energy to grow and harvest. This

This is a biogas factory. Biogas is often made when tiny living things break down animal wastes. The by-product is biogas, which can be used as fuel.

energy usually comes from fossil fuels. Corn also takes a lot of land to grow, which can lead to the destruction of wild habitats. Scientists are working on ways to make bioalcohol from energy-efficient nonfood plants, such as grass and farming waste.

Biodiesel is produced from animal fats and plant oils. If combined with diesel oil, it can be used in ordinary

IT'S A FACT!

Did you know that you can power a car with french fry oil? "Veggie cars" use oil recycled from restaurant deep fryers to power diesel engines.

diesel engines. Some vehicles are made to run on this biofuel. Biodiesel releases less pollution into the air than petroleum does. It is often made by recycling leftover oil from meat processing and fast-food restaurants.

Unfortunately, there is not enough of this waste oil to go around, so biodiesel is also made by growing crops such as soybeans. This creates some of the same problems that corn ethanol does.

This car has a special engine that runs on bioethanol. It was presented at an agricultural fair in France in 2007.

Biogas is produced when organic matter is turned into methane gas. Biogas can be made from plants. It can also be made from sewage and animal **manure**. These are all renewable resources. Cars need special fuel systems to run on biogas.

A Green School Bus?

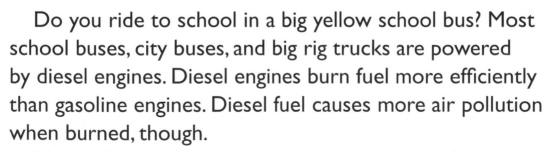

Students at South Shore Public Charter School, in Norwell, Massachusetts, stand in front of their school's hybrid bus.

Do you ride to school in a big yellow school bus? Most school buses, city buses, and big rig trucks are powered by diesel engines. Diesel engines burn fuel more efficiently than gasoline engines. Diesel fuel causes more air pollution when burned, though.

Many school districts and cities are trying to clean up the air in their communities by choosing Earth-friendly transportation. Adding **filters** to buses cleans up the exhaust that the engines produce. Using low-sulfur fuel also helps reduce the polluting **emissions**.

Some places are taking green power even further. The Los Angeles Unified School District replaced its old school buses with propane vehicles. These buses are more energy efficient and cause less air

Here is one of London's red double-decker buses. The new hybrid buses are part of a plan to cut back on air pollution in the city.

pollution. In London, the famous red double-decker buses will now run on hybrid engines. The new engines will make the buses 40 percent more fuel efficient than the old ones. New York City is working to be Earth friendlier, too. The city just added 1,171 hybrid electric buses to their fleet of public buses!

This is one of Minneapolis's hybrid electric buses. Since 2002, this city has put more than 70 hybrid-electric buses on the roads.

All Together Now

Taking public transportation is a much Earth-friendlier choice than driving, even if that public transportation does not use any green technology. If more people travel in one vehicle, less energy gets used to move

Many highways have special lanes marked with diamonds that are for drivers who carpool. Carpooling is a great way to help Earth if you cannot use public transportation.

them. Fewer cars will be on the road, and less fuel will be burned. In the United States, public transportation saves 1.4 billion gallons (5.3 billion l) of gas every year and reduces carbon dioxide emissions by more than 7.4 million tons (6.7 million t)!

Riding the subway to work is an Earth-friendly choice. Talk to your parents about whether public transportation is an option for them.

Buses can usually carry up to 60 passengers, which could mean 60 fewer cars on the road. Subway trains, however, can carry up to 10,000 passengers an hour! Subways are a great way to travel. Because they travel underground, they do not create more traffic in the

Tell everyone you know who has a car to check their tire pressure. Keeping car tires full of air means cars go farther on less gas, and that is good sense for every wallet.

Some places have boats that can take people where they need to go. In New York City, the Staten Island Ferry, shown here, carries people from Staten Island to Manhattan.

streets. Subways, which run on electricity, also use less fuel and produce less carbon dioxide per passenger than buses. Cities that are located on large bodies of water can also provide public transportation through ferry boats.

Airplanes are not a form of public transportation. They do carry a lot of people all over the world, though.

Planes use a great deal of petroleum to lift their heavy loads into the sky. They also release pollution high in the atmosphere, where it can be even more harmful. Many airlines are now trying to find ways to become Earth friendlier. Some airlines are trying to use biofuels in their planes. Others are trying to lighten their loads by using materials that weigh less to build planes.

This is Boeing's Dreamliner. The plane is made of light materials that save the airline about 20 percent in fuel costs.

Move Your Body

Using your feet is the Earth-friendliest way to travel! Walking or biking places instead of driving is great for your body, since it helps give you the exercise you need. It is also great for the environment because it uses no fossil fuels at all and creates no air pollution.

Walking to school is one way to help Earth. Getting a ride from a parent means she is using gas and polluting the air.

Traveling by bike can sometimes be even faster than driving a car since you are less likely to get stuck in a traffic jam or spend time looking for a parking spot. Riding through traffic in big, crowded cities can

Many cities have bike lanes that make it easier and safer for people to ride their bikes.

be dangerous, however. To get more people to ride bicycles instead of driving, many cities are making biking safer by adding special lanes where cars are not allowed to city streets.

Where Do We Go from Here?

This man who works for a Japanese automaker shows a new fuel cell technology his company is working on. It is able to put out as much energy as a hydrogen fuel cell.

The technology for Earth-friendly transportation keeps getting better. The next step for green cars might be hydrogen fuel cells, which produce electricity within the car by combining the chemical hydrogen with oxygen

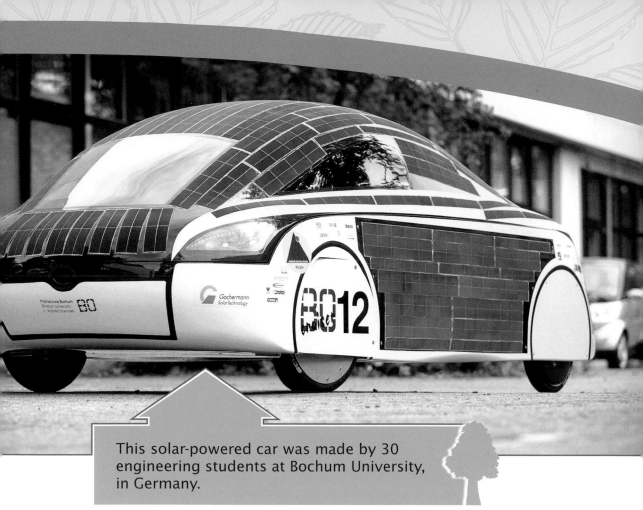

This solar-powered car was made by 30 engineering students at Bochum University, in Germany.

from the air. Hydrogen fuel cells create energy without **combustion**, so they produce no harmful emissions. Hydrogen is also two to three times more energy efficient as a fuel than gasoline. Scientists are currently working on safe ways to produce and store hydrogen fuel. Solar cars, which would turn energy from the Sun into electricity to power the battery, might also be on their way.

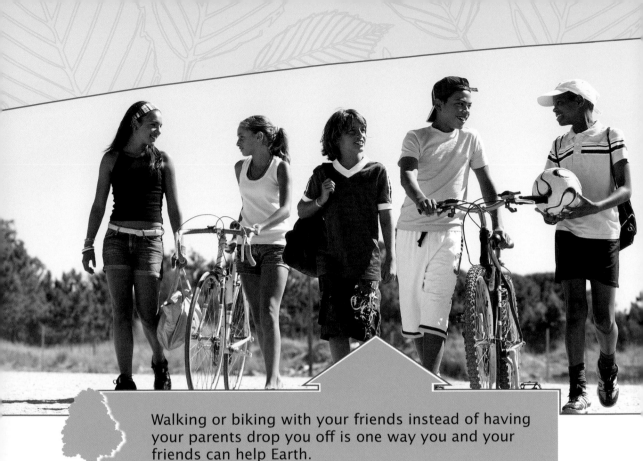

Walking or biking with your friends instead of having your parents drop you off is one way you and your friends can help Earth.

In the meantime, the U.S. government has said that ordinary vehicles must become more fuel efficient and cleaner. You help Earth every time you walk or ride your bike instead of having your parents drive you somewhere. Ask your parents to carpool if they do not already. Take public transportation instead of a car where it is possible. Everybody has the power to make responsible choices. Everyone can be a friend to Earth!

GLOSSARY

battery (BA-tuh-ree) A thing in which energy is stored.

carbon dioxide (KAR-bin dy-OK-syd) An odorless, colorless gas. People breathe out carbon dioxide.

combustion (kom-BUS-chun) Burning.

efficiently (ih-FIH-shent-lee) Done in the quickest, best way possible.

emissions (ee-MIH-shunz) Things, such as pollution or gases, put into the air by something, such as an engine.

environment (en-VY-ern-ment) Everything around human beings and other living things and everything that makes it possible for them to live.

fermenting (fur-MENT-ing) Changing in a way that makes gas bubbles.

filters (FIL-turz) Things that takes unwanted things from water or air.

fuel (FYOO-el) Something burned to make heat or power.

hybrid cars (HY-brud KAHRZ) Cars that have an engine that runs on gasoline and a motor that runs on electricity.

manure (muh-NOOR) Animal waste.

outlet (OWT-let) A place to plug something in to give it an electric charge.

resources (REE-sawrs-ez) Supplies or sources of energy or useful things.

sustainable (suh-STAY-nuh-bel) Able to be kept going.

transportation (tranz-per-TAY-shun) A way of traveling from one place to another.

vehicles (VEE-uh-kulz) Means of moving or carrying things.

INDEX

WEB SITES

Due to the changing nature of Internet links, PowerKids Press has developed an online list of Web sites related to the subject of this book. This site is updated regularly. Please use this link to access the list:
www.powerkidslinks.com/hbef/trans/